WINTER STORY

Jill Barklem

ATHENEUM BOOKS FOR YOUNG READERS

For David

Atheneum Books for Young Readers
An imprint of Simon & Schuster Children's Publishing Division
1230 Avenue of the Americas
New York, New York 10020

First published in Great Britain by HarperCollins Publishers Ltd
First United States Edition, 1999

Printed in China

10 9 8 7 6 5 4 3 2 1
Library of Congress Catalog Card Number: 99-60146

ISBN 0-689-83057-2

BRAMBLY HEDGE

For many generations, families of mice have made
their homes in the roots and trunks
of the trees of Brambly Hedge,
a dense and tangled hedgerow
that borders the field on the
other side of the stream.

The Brambly Hedge mice lead
busy lives. During the fine weather,
they collect flowers, fruits, berries and nuts from the
Hedge and surrounding fields, and prepare
delicious jams, pickles and preserves that
are kept safely in the Store Stump for
the winter months ahead.

Although the mice work hard, they make
time for fun too. All through the year, they
mark the seasons with feasts and festivities and, whether
it be a little mouse's birthday, an eagerly awaited wedding
or the first day of spring, the mice
welcome the opportunity
to meet and celebrate.

It was the middle of winter. The sun had just set and it was very, very cold. An icy wind was blowing from the East, and the wind promised snow.

Deep in the dark roots of Brambly Hedge, tiny lights appeared as lamps were lit in the windows.

More little lights could be seen leaving the Store Stump, moving hastily along the hedgerow and disappearing into holes hidden in the twisty roots. The mice had smelled snow in the air and were all hurrying home to a nice hot supper by the fire.

Mr. Apple, warden of the Store Stump, was the last to leave for home. By the time he reached Crabapple Cottage, the first flakes were beginning to fall.

"Is that you, dear?" called Mrs. Apple as he let himself in through the front door. Delicious smells wafted down from the kitchen. Mrs. Apple had spent the afternoon baking pies, cakes and puddings for the cold days to come. She drew two armchairs up to the fire and brought in their supper on a tray.

There was a lot of noise coming from the
hornbeam tree next door. The Toadflax children
had never seen snow before.

"It's snowing! It really is SNOWING!"
squeaked the two boys, Wilfred and Teasel.

They chased their sisters, Clover and Catkin, around
the kitchen, with pawfuls of snow scooped from
the windowsill.

"Suppertime!" called Mrs. Toadflax firmly,
ladling hot chestnut soup into four small bowls.

After supper the children were sent off to bed, but they were far too excited to sleep. As soon as the grown-ups were safely occupied downstairs, they climbed out of their bunk beds to watch the snowflakes falling past the window.

"Tobogganing tomorrow," said Wilfred.

"Snow pancakes for tea," said Clover.

"We'll make a snow mouse," said Catkin.

"And I'll knock it down!" said Teasel, pushing the girls off their chair.

Next morning the mice along the hedgerow
woke to find their windows half-blocked by snow.
Mrs. Apple had to stand on tiptoes on the
kitchen table to see out. And what a sight met

her eyes! The fields were covered with a thick white blanket of snow, and all the paths and plants had disappeared beneath it.

When the Toadflax family went down to
breakfast, they found the kitchen dark and still.
Mrs. Toadflax put fresh wood on the fire and
set Clover to work with the toasting fork. Soon
they were all sitting round the table, eating hot
buttered toast, drinking blackberry leaf tea and
making plans for the day ahead.

The snow was thicker than the mice had
expected. All the downstairs windows along the
hedgerow were covered with snow, and many of
the upper ones, too, were hidden in deep drifts.

The mice leaned out of their bedroom windows
to wave and call to their friends.

"Enough for a Snow Ball, wouldn't you say?"
called Mr. Toadflax to Mrs. Apple.

"A Snow Ball!" echoed the little mice gleefully.

Every family along the hedgerow kept shovels, maps and ropes in a special cupboard by the front door, and after breakfast the mice dug tunnels from tree to tree, linking them all to the Store Stump. Teasel and Wilfred were sent down to help, but they soon found that it was much more fun to throw snow at each other and so were sent home again.

Lord Woodmouse dug his way through to old
Mrs. Eyebright and helped her to light a fire.

"I haven't seen snow like this since I was
young," she sighed. "The last Snow Ball was
held in the year Mr. Eyebright and I were married.
I'm the only one left who can remember it now."

When the tunnels were finished, all the mice
gathered noisily in the Store Stump Hall.

Mrs. Apple took some seed cake from the cupboard and prepared a jug of acorn coffee. The mice helped themselves and gathered around Mr. Apple, who held up a paw for silence. "Lord Woodmouse and I have agreed," he said when they were quiet, "that we should follow in the tradition of our forefathers." He cleared his throat nervously, straightened his whiskers and recited,

> *"When the snows are lying deep,*
> *When the field has gone to sleep,*
> *When the blackthorn turns to white,*
> *And frosty stars bejewel the night,*
> *When summer streams are turned to ice,*
> *A Snow Ball warms the hearts of mice.*

"Friends, I declare that a Snow Ball will take place at dusk tonight in the Ice Hall."

"Where's that?" whispered Clover, as the mice clapped and cheered.

"Wait and see!" replied Mrs. Apple. "You come home with me and help prepare the feast."

There was a deep drift of snow banked against the Store Stump, and the elder mice, after discussion, declared it to be "just right" for the Ice Hall. Mr. Apple dug the first tunnel to check that the snow was firm.

"It's perfect!" he called back from the middle of the drift. The mice picked up their shovels and the digging began.

The snow was dug from inside the drift, piled into carts and taken down to the stream. Wilfred and Teasel helped enthusiastically, but they were sent home again when Mr. Apple caught them putting icicles down Catkin's dress.

The middle of the drift was carefully hollowed out. Mr. Apple inspected the roof very thoroughly to make sure that it was safe.

"Safe as the Store Stump!" he declared.

All the kitchens along Brambly Hedge were
warm and busy. Hot soups, punches and puddings
bubbled and in the ovens pies browned and sizzled.
Clover and Catkin helped Mrs. Apple string

crabapples to roast over the fire. The boys
had to sit and watch because they ate too many.
"It's not that I mind, dears, but we must have
SOME left for the punch!"

The glowworms were put in charge of the lighting. Mr. Toadflax fetched them early from the bank at the end of the Hedge, for Mrs. Apple had insisted that they should have a good supper before their long night's work began.

By teatime the Hall was finished. The ice columns and carvings sparkled in the blue-green light and the polished dance floor shone. Tables were set at the end of the Hall and eager cooks bustled in from their kitchens with baskets of food.

The children decorated a small raised platform with sprays of holly while Basil, the keeper of the hedgerow wines, set out some chairs for the musicians.

When all was done, the mice admired their handiwork and went home to wash and change.

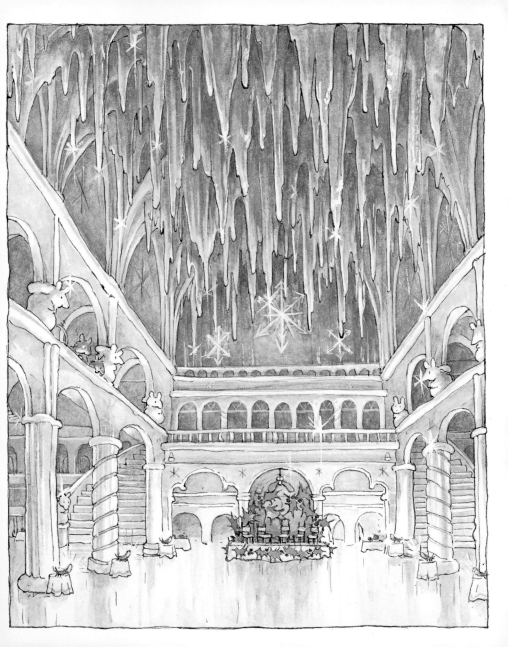

As muffs and mufflers were left at the door, it was clear that all the mice had dressed up for the grand occasion. Wilfred and Teasel crept under a table to watch, and every now and then a little paw appeared and a cream cake disappeared.

Basil struck up a jolly tune on his violin and the

dancing began. All the dances were very fast and
twirly and were made even faster by the slippery
ice floor. Wilfred and Teasel whirled their sisters
round so quickly that their paws left the ground.

"I don't feel very well," said Clover, looking
rather green.

Mrs. Apple stood on a chair and banged two saucepan lids together.

"Supper is served," she called.

The eating and drinking and dancing carried on late into the night. At midnight, all the hedgerow children were taken home to bed.

As soon as they were safely tucked up, their parents returned to the Ball. Basil made some hot blackberry punch and the dancing got faster and faster.

The Snow Ball went on until dawn.

The musicians were tired. The ice columns began to drip. The sleepy mice could dance no more. They wandered home through the snow tunnels, climbed the stairs and crept into their warm beds.

Outside the window, the snow had started to fall again.

But every mouse in Brambly Hedge was fast asleep.